Growing Vegetable Soup

Written and illustrated by Lois Ehlert

Voyager Books · Harcourt, Inc.

San Diego   New York   London

DEDICATED TO MY FELLOW GARDENERS:
GLADYS, HARRY, JOHN, AND JAN

Voyager Books is a registered trademark of Harcourt, Inc.

The Library of Congress has cataloged the
hardcover edition as follows:
Ehlert, Lois.
Growing vegetable soup.
Summary: A father and child grow vegetables and then
make them into a soup.
[1. Vegetable gardening—Fiction.   2. Soups—Fiction.]
I. Title.
PZ7.E44Gr 1987   [E]   86-22812
ISBN 0-15-232575-1
ISBN 0-15-232580-8 pb
ISBN 0-15-232581-6 oversize pb

Y X W V U T S
Printed in Singapore

Dad says we are going to grow vegetable soup.

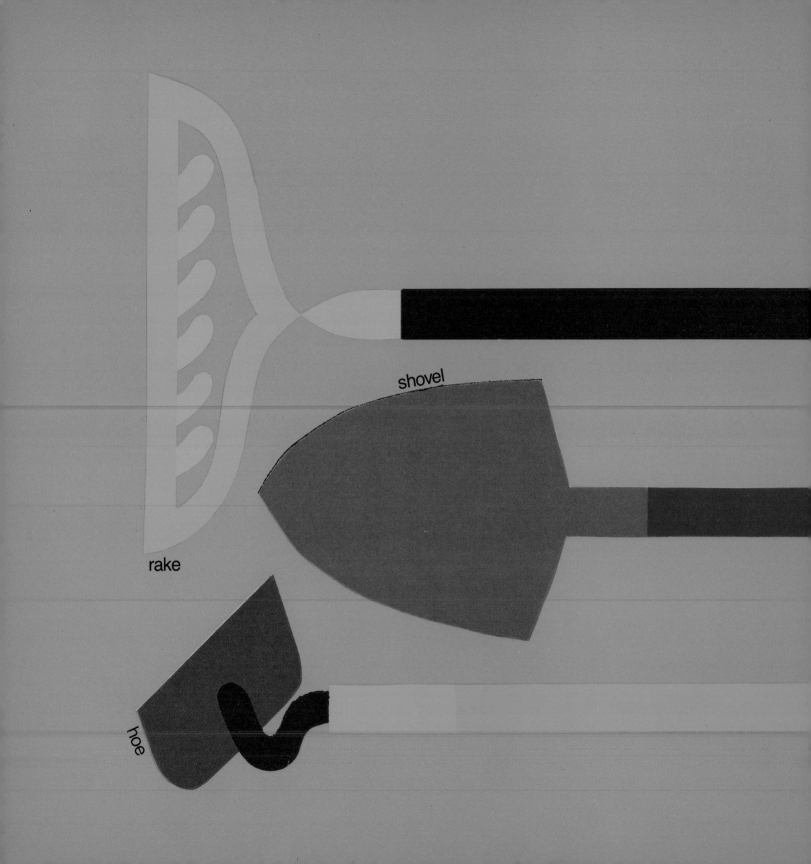

rake

shovel

hoe

We're ready to work, and our tools are ready, too.

We are planting

seed package

soil

hole

the seeds,

garden glove

green bean
seed

pea
seed

corn
seed

zucchini squash
seed

carrot
seeds

and all the sprouts,

broccoli

TOMATO

potato eyes

trowel

PEPPER

CABBAGE

set onions

peat moss pot

TOMATO

POTATO

GREEN BEAN

CARROT

CABBAGE

watering can

and giving them water,

PEPPER

ZUCCHINI SQUASH

PEA

ONION

BROCCOLI

CORN

water

and waiting for warm sun to make them grow,

and grow,

soil

ZUCCHINI SQUASH

ONION

POTATO

PEA

CARROT

CORN

weed

and grow into plants.

net

stake

PEA

soil

squash
bud

squash
blossom

ZUCCHINI SQUASH

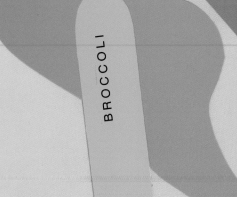

worm

BROCCOLI

We watch

over them and weed,

hand
grubber

GREEN BEAN

until the vegetables are ready for us to pick

TOMATO

pepper

corn

hand basket

spading
fork

or dig up

carrot

potato

bushel basket

and carry home.
Then we wash them

cabbage

onion

pail

and cut them and put them in a pot of water,

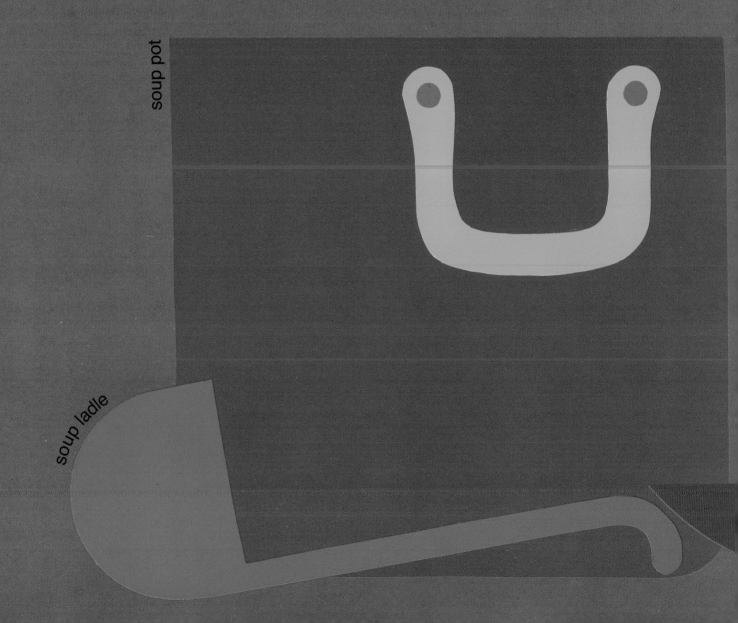

soup pot

soup ladle

carrot

corn

onion

zucchini squash

tomato

pea

broccoli

potato

pepper

green bean

knife

cabbage

and cook them into vegetable soup!

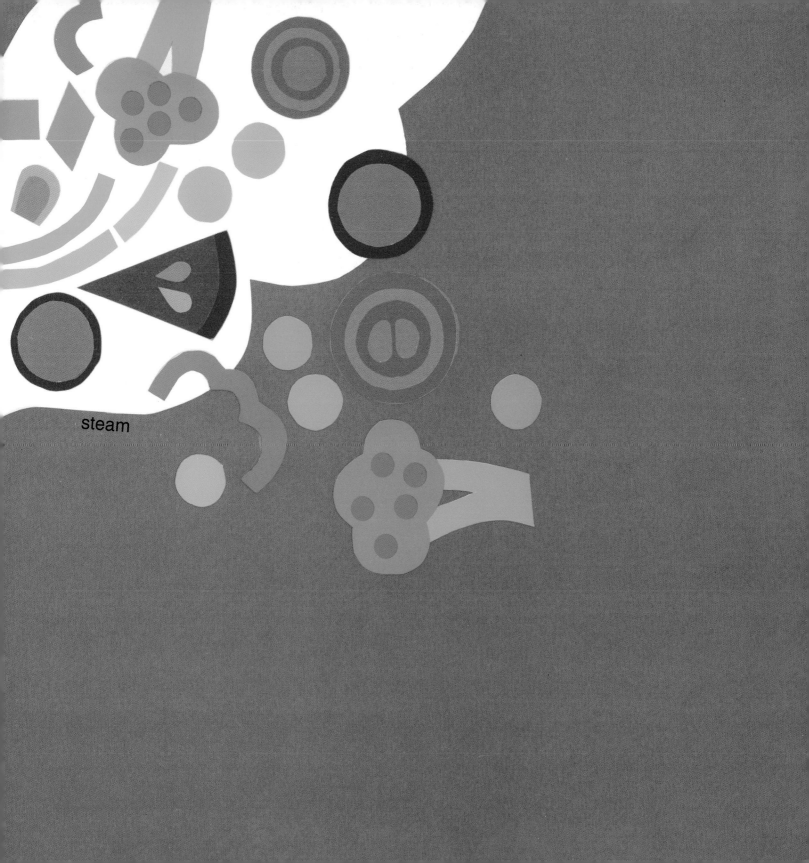

steam

soupspoon

soup bowl

At last it's time
to eat it all up!

It was the
best soup ever…

and we can
grow it again
next year.